THE
HAPPY DAY

By
RUTH KRAUSS
Pictures by
MARC SIMONT

HarperCollins*Publishers*

THE
HAPPY DAY

Snow is falling.

The field mice are sleeping,

the bears are sleeping,

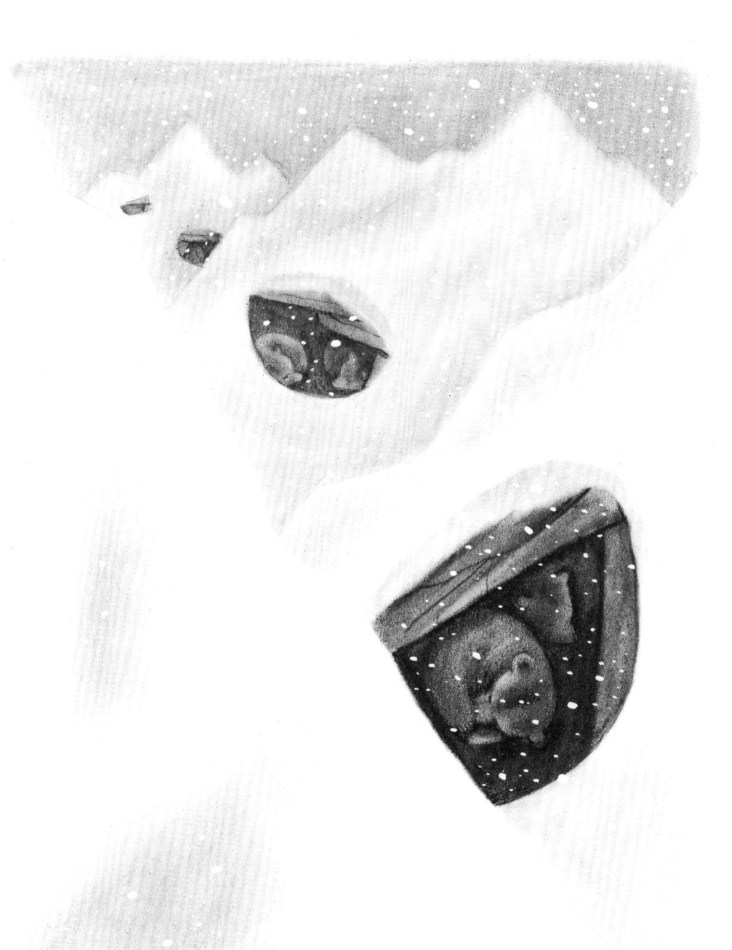

the little snails sleep in their shells;

and the squirrels sleep in the trees,

the ground hogs sleep in the ground.

Now, they open their eyes. They sniff.

The field mice sniff,

the bears sniff,

the little snails sniff in their shells;

and the squirrels sniff in the trees,

the ground hogs sniff in the ground.

They sniff. They run.

The field mice run,

the bears run,

the little snails run with their shells,

and the squirrels run out of the trees,

the ground hogs run out of the ground.

They sniff. They run.

They run. They sniff.

They sniff. They run. They stop.

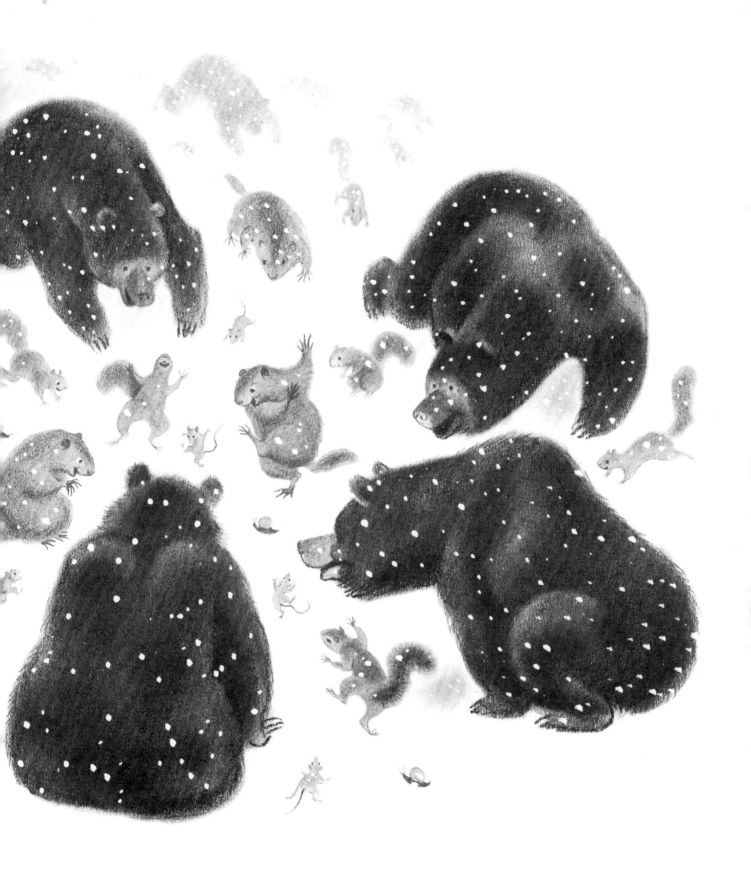

They stop. They laugh.
They laugh. They dance.

They cry, "Oh!
A flower is growing in the snow."